LOST

CAT

"NIBLET"

BUZZ DILLA APT 2B

NIBLET

*For Susan and
Farmer John
and all the cats who
wandered into our lives*

Dial Books for Young Readers
Penguin Young Readers Group
An imprint of Penguin Random House LLC
375 Hudson Street, New York, NY 10014

Copyright © 2018 by Zachariah OHora

ISBN 9780735227910 • Printed in China • 10 9 8 7 6 5 4 3 2 1

Design by Lily Malcom • Text set in Rockwell

The artwork was created using acrylic paint on Stonehenge printmaking paper.

& RALPH

ZACHARIAH OHORA

Dial Books for Young Readers

This is Gemma and Ralph.

This is Dilla and Niblet.

They all live in the same building.
Two of them know this, but two do not.

Can you guess who *does* know?

You guessed it! Ralph and Niblet!
They talk together on the phone all day.

When they run out of things to say . . .

they share the sun.

One day Ralph found a way to visit Niblet.

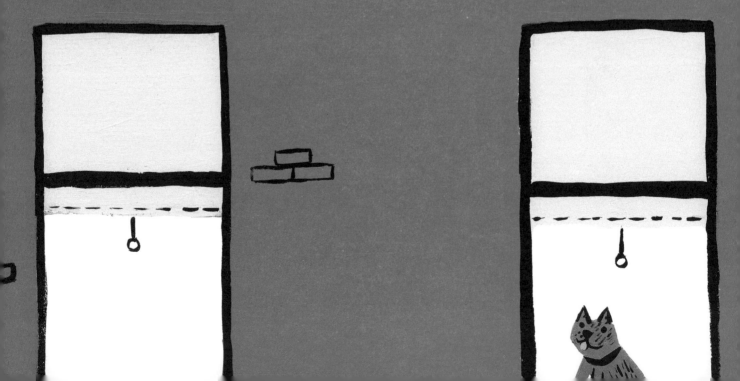

And Niblet found a way to visit Ralph.

Except when Niblet got to Ralph's, no one was home.
I'll just wait for Ralph, he thought.

When Ralph got to Niblet's, nobody was home there, either.
He probably just stepped into the litter box, **thought Ralph.**

When Gemma came home after school she scooped up
Ralph to hug him. But Niblet did not want to be hugged.

When Dilla came home from school he got out
Niblet's favorite toy. But Ralph did not want to play.

There was something not quite right about Ralph.
Gemma decided to run a test.

She put headphones on Ralph and played his favorite song.
But Niblet hated it!

"THIS IS A FAKE RALPH!" Gemma shouted
"RALPH HAS BEEN CLONED AND REPLACED!"

"Maybe he's just tired," yawned her dad.
"It's time for bed."

HIISSSSSSSSSSS!!

Dilla knew there was something off about Niblet. So he tried a little experiment.

"THIS IS NOT NIBLET!" he shouted. "NIBLET LOVES CHIPS AND THIS CAT DOES NOT!"

SNIFF SNIFF

"You think someone snuck in here and replaced
Niblet with another cat?" laughed his mom.
"Time for bed, Detective Dilla!"

All night Gemma wondered what had happened to Ralph.

And all night Dilla worried about what had happened to Niblet.

Fake Ralph was nice enough,
but Gemma missed the real Ralph.
Her dad was not convinced he was gone.
It was time to take matters into her own hands.

**Dilla liked Not Niblet, but he missed the real Niblet.
His mom didn't believe that Niblet was missing.
It was time to investigate.**

Gemma looked everywhere for Ralph.

Dilla did the same for Niblet. Until . . .

"You mean Fake Ralph?" yelped Gemma.

"You mean Not Niblet?" asked Dilla.
Finally, the mystery was solved!

Back home Dilla and Gemma met in the hallway
with Niblet and Ralph. Niblet was so happy to see
Dilla he didn't mind being hugged.

Ralph was so happy to see Gemma
he leaped straight into her arms.
Gemma and her dad invited everyone for dinner.

Now everyone was where they belonged . . .

Together!